Albany Public Library
Albany, N

W9-BHN-940

HAUNTED STATES
of
AMERICA

CURSE
→ of the ←
DEAD-EYED
DOLL

Curse of the Dead-Eyed Doll © 2020 by North Star Editions, Mendota Heights, MN 55120. All rights reserved. No part of this book may be used or reproduced in any manner whatsoever, including internet usage, without written permission from the copyright owner, except in the case of brief quotations embodied in critical articles and reviews.

Book design by Sarah Taplin
Cover illustration by Maggie Ivy
Interior illustrations by Clonefront Entertainment (Beehive Illustration)

Published in the United States by Jolly Fish Press, an imprint of North Star Editions, Inc.

First Edition
First Printing, 2019

This is a work of fiction. Names, characters, places, and incidents are either the product of the author's imagination or are used fictitiously, and any resemblance to actual persons living or dead, business establishments, events, or locales is entirely coincidental.

Library of Congress Cataloging-in-Publication Data
Names: Troupe, Thomas Kingsley, author.
Title: Curse of the dead-eyed doll / by Thomas Kingsley Troupe.
Description: First edition. | Mendota Heights, MN : Jolly Fish Press, [2020] | Series: Haunted States of America | Summary: "Strange things start to happen to Al after visiting a Key West, Florida, museum and taking a photograph of Robert the Doll"— Provided by publisher.
Identifiers: LCCN 2018060106 (print) | LCCN 2019003419 (ebook) | ISBN 9781631633492 (ebook) | ISBN 9781631633478 (hardcover) | ISBN 9781631633485 (pbk.)
Subjects: | CYAC: Blessing and cursing—Fiction. | Haunted places—Fiction. | Dolls—Fiction. | Photographs—Fiction. | Horror stories. | Key West (Fla.)—Fiction. | LCGFT: Fiction.
Classification: LCC PZ7.T7538 (ebook) | LCC PZ7.T7538 Cu 2019 (print) | DDC [Fic]—dc23
LC record available at https://lccn.loc.gov/2018060106

Jolly Fish Press
North Star Editions, Inc.
2297 Waters Drive
Mendota Heights, MN 55120
www.jollyfishpress.com

Printed in the United States of America

HAUNTED STATES
of
AMERICA

CURSE
— of the —
DEAD-EYED
DOLL

THOMAS KINGSLEY TROUPE

JOLLY
FiSH
PRESS
Mendota Heights, Minnesota

CHAPTER 1

FIELD TRIP

"Slow down, son," Al's dad cried. "You're going to choke!"

Alejandro Padilla looked up from his bowl of cereal as a stream of milk dribbled down his chin. His dad was about to bite into a piece of toast with egg and ham on top. Marco, his older brother, shook his head.

"You always eat like it's your last meal, Al," Marco added.

"Forry," Al replied.

"Not with your mouth full," Dad said.

Al chewed, swallowed, and wiped the milk from his face.

"Try that again?" his dad asked. He took a slow sip of his coffee.

"I said sorry," Al said, digging up another heaping spoonful of Honey O's. "I'm just hungry, I guess."

"Well, when you choke to death, being hungry will cease to be a problem," Dad said.

"There's a nice thought to start out the day," Al

grumbled, spooning up a much smaller portion of his breakfast.

Al had thought his brother and dad might ease up on him a bit once he became a teenager. But after turning thirteen over three months ago, he realized that wasn't going to happen.

"Your history paper," Dad began. "Is it finished?"

"No, Mrs. Crowley changed the due date to Friday,"

Al replied. "She forgot we've got that field trip today. I'll work on it tonight after school, no sweat."

Marco brought his empty dish to the sink. He drank the last of his orange juice and rinsed the glass out.

"Field trip?" Marco asked. "Where are you guys going?"

Al shrugged. "Some fort museum or something."

Marco nodded and smirked. "The Fort East Martello Museum," he said. "We went there when I was a kid too."

Al snorted then mumbled, "You're sixteen years old, not thirty."

Marco ignored him.

Al asked, "Is it any good?"

Marco shrugged. "It's okay, I guess. They have a little bit of everything there. A bunch of Civil War antiques and some guy's art he made out of junk."

"Well, that sounds great," Al said, failing to muster up excitement.

Actually, Al didn't care where they were going. The museum could be filled with pencil shavings for all he cared. He was just happy to get out of school for a good chunk of the day.

"Oh, there's one other thing," Marco said, leaning against the kitchen counter. "They've got this weird-looking doll there. It's supposed to be haunted or cursed."

"Cursed?"

"Yeah," Marco replied. "They make a pretty big deal about it. I bet it's the only reason people go there."

"That's absurd," their dad said, waving his hand at Marco. "Complete nonsense!"

Al couldn't help but smile. He liked seeing his dad get worked up.

"You don't believe in that stuff, Dad?" Al asked.

"Ghosts and haunted toys? That's for the movies," he responded, finishing his toast. "The idiots who believe in that stuff are as empty-headed as those dolls."

Al couldn't agree more. There were tons of TV shows about people running around in the dark, looking for ghosts. Those shows seemed totally fake to him, yet they were pretty popular among his friends at school.

Guess they're idiots too, Al thought. *According to my dad, at least.*

"Like I said," Marco replied. "They've got a little bit of everything."

After stealing one more handful of cereal from the box still sitting on the table, Al grabbed his backpack and skateboard.

"Have a good time at the doll museum," Dad said, waving Al over for a hug.

Al let his dad wrap his arms around him and clap him on the back.

"Thanks, Dad," he said, his voice muffled by the hug.

"And as soon as you get home tonight?"

"History paper," Al said. "I know, I know."

———————

A little before 9:30 a.m., a school bus packed with sixty eighth-graders pulled into the parking lot of the Fort East Martello Museum. Al studied the brick building as the bus slowed down in front of it. Next to him, Al's friend Selma peered over his shoulder.

Al's family had passed the fort countless times driving on Highway A1A, but he'd never paid much attention to it. There was an old bell in front of the building, along with a giant, black boat anchor that was partially buried in the rocks. Next to the sidewalk leading into the museum was a flagpole with an American flag hoisted to the top.

A sign to the right of the building announced what the eighth-grade students of Gulf View Middle School could expect inside:

FORT EAST MARTELLO MUSEUM
CIVIL WAR-ERA FORT

LEARN ABOUT:
Key West Industries
Robert the Doll
Local Folk Art
Citadel Tower
Military History
Museum Store

"Wow," Al said. "The doll got second billing."

"The doll?" Selma asked. "What are you talking about?"

He pointed at the sign. "Marco said there's a doll in there that's supposed to be super creepy and haunted," Al said. "But really, how scary can a doll named Robert be?"

Selma shivered a bit. "Dolls creep me out," she admitted. "I never even had any growing up. My parents said I would cry anytime my sisters played with them."

"Sure, dolls can be creepy," Al said. "But Robert? Kind of a dumb name for a doll if you ask me."

Once the bus stopped, Mrs. Crowley stood up and

announced the plan for the day. First, they would go on a tour of the museum and learn about the Civil War relics. From there, they'd break for lunch and then get an hour or so to explore the museum on their own.

The bus doors opened, and the students spilled out. They followed Mrs. Crowley to the front door, where their tour guide, a middle-aged man named Corey, introduced himself. As the students waited to go inside, Al looked at a poster beside the door.

"Check it out," he whispered to Selma.

"Oh, no," Selma said with a gasp. She immediately looked away from the poster. "Nope. No thanks."

The mounted frame beside them displayed a black poster with a faded picture of a doll. Above the doll's head in thin, shaky letters were the words *ROBERT DID IT*.

What'd he do? Al wondered. *Get people to believe he's haunted?*

Beside him, Selma was still turned away from the poster.

"What, you don't want to see the most haunted doll in the world?" Al asked. "Or at least in Key West, Florida?"

"Stop it," Selma said, giving him a playful shove.

Al listened to his classmates' growing excitement

over the old doll. Some of them posed near the poster and took photos on their phones.

Within a few minutes, the group moved inside the dark entryway and into a gift shop. It reminded Al of the countless amusement park rides he'd tried whenever they visited Orlando. The exits always managed to dump riders off at a store loaded with stuff for them to buy.

"This place hits you with the gifts right away," Al said.

"Good thing you brought your wallet," Selma joked.

Al looked around. Museum-themed tote bags, American flags, books, mugs, and anything else one might want from a Civil War museum filled the room. There were even some antique-looking items spread about.

Al burst out laughing when he came to one section of the shop.

"What's so funny?" Selma asked from a few feet away. She was examining an iron rooster with a teal-colored tail.

"Don't come over here," Al warned. "Unless you want nightmares."

Inside a large green dollhouse was a display of Robert the Doll collectibles. There were buttons, magnets, and postcards with the doll's face printed on them.

But what really got Al's attention were the miniature stuffed dolls.

"You've got to be kidding me," he whispered. Miniature Robert sat in a tiny wooden chair. He was dressed in what looked like a sailor suit and had a small stuffed dog under his arm. In Al's opinion, the miniature doll was a much cuter version of what he saw on the poster at the museum entrance.

The creepy little guy really is the big attraction here, I guess, Al thought.

"Interested in getting a Robert of your own?" an older woman asked. She was hanging T-shirts on a rack. She took out one of the shirts and swapped it out with another one.

"No, no," Al said. "I'm good. But do people actually buy these?"

The lady laughed. "Like you wouldn't believe," she said. "They're probably one of our most popular items."

Al looked at the picture on the cover of a book about Robert and shook his head.

"He's not even all that scary looking," he said. "I guess I expected him to look like—"

"Something out of the movies?" the woman asked. "I hear that quite a bit. But when you see him in real life, you'll see what all the fuss is about." The woman winked, making Al think she was just kidding.

Al spotted Selma waving him over to join their class, who was now walking into the main part of the museum. He nodded quickly, knowing he had to get moving but wanting to finish his conversation.

"Has anything spooky happened while you've worked here?" Al asked. He might not have believed in that stuff, but he was fascinated by people who did.

"Oh, sure," the lady said, straightening out a stack of books on a nearby table. "Robert does all kinds of things, especially if he doesn't like you. I do my best to stay on his good side."

A shiver ran up Al's neck. He glanced down to see the hairs on his arms stick straight up and goose bumps pepper his skin.

"Al!" Selma whispered from a rotating postcard display.

She was frantically waving him over. Their teacher and the rest of the class had already moved on.

"We have to go!" she hissed. "They're already starting!"

As Al turned to say goodbye to the woman, he found she was no longer standing there.

———————

The museum tour was actually a lot more interesting than Al thought it would be. Corey explained that the fort was built during the Civil War in preparation for a battle that never ended up happening. The construction was never completed, and the fort was left abandoned when there was no use for it. In 1950, a historical society cleared out the debris and turned the fort into a museum.

Corey took the group through long passages called "casemates" that surrounded the inner portion of the fort. They read about a number of Civil War relics, learned about the Key West wrecking industry, and saw some of the things that had been found on sunken ships. There was also an art display featuring the works of a man named Stanley Papio, who created large sculptures out of old metal junk.

After a quick lunch break outside, Corey asked for the class's attention.

"Thanks for pretending to listen to the first part of the tour," Corey said with a smile. A handful of Al's classmates laughed. "I know the real reason you were excited to come to Fort East Martello," he continued. "You probably read about him and saw his picture online.

It's time to take you to the most popular artifact in the museum."

Here we go, Al thought. He watched as some of his classmates squirmed with excitement. Selma wasn't one of them.

"Do we have to?" she whispered to him.

"C'mon," Al said with a smirk. "It's just a doll in a sailor suit. What's the worst that can happen?"

CHAPTER 2

HELLO, ROBBY

Al and Selma followed the rest of the group down a white corridor inside one of the fort's casements. They passed a number of antiques displayed along the sides of the walkway, including an old wooden piano and a white dollhouse inside of a clear plastic case. Closer to a set of open double doors, Al saw a stone wheel set into a stand. Apparently it was used to sharpen knives back in the old days.

Corey stopped the group in front of the doors. "Just inside this section of the casement is the area we call Robert's Room," he said. "But before we go in, I need to warn you about something. You are welcome to take photos of Robert the Doll, but only on one condition."

The room was silent, waiting for Corey to explain what the one condition was.

"You need to ask his permission," Corey said, his face serious.

Al almost laughed out loud. The guy was a really

good actor. He was a funny, friendly tour guide one minute, then completely stern the next.

"Really? What happens if we don't?" Rachel asked from the edge of the group.

"He gets upset," Corey said. "There have been thousands of people who haven't heeded our warnings, and nothing but bad luck follows them."

"You mean like a curse?" Patrick, a guy from Al's football team, blurted.

"Exactly like a curse," Corey said. "Robert thinks it's rude to take his picture without asking. We've heard about the things that have happened to people who don't follow the rule, and . . . they're not good."

Al leaned closer to Selma and whispered in her ear.

"I don't believe this garbage. Do you?"

"Not sure," Selma said. "But what if it's true?"

"It's just a way to keep people interested in the place," Al said. "If the museum's only big attraction is the old stuff and the history of pillaging shipwrecks, you think anyone would come here?"

Selma let out a shaky exhale. Al could tell she was nervous about the whole thing.

"Where did Robert come from?" Nadia, one of Selma's friends, asked.

Corey clasped his hands together in front of his chest and smiled.

"I'm so glad you asked," he said. "Follow me into Robert's Room, and I'll tell you all about him. I think he likes hearing his own story."

Sure he does, Al thought, and rolled his eyes.

The group followed Corey into the darker room. There, sitting on a chair atop a square, light gray pedestal, and completely enclosed in a clear plastic display case, was Robert the Doll.

Al couldn't quite explain it, but it felt like the energy was sucked right out of the room. He guessed it was everyone inhaling fear at the same time.

Corey walked over next to Robert's casement and motioned to the doll.

"Everyone," Corey said. "I'd like to introduce you to Robert."

Al heard a few of his classmates murmur *Hi, Robert* like little kids greeting their teacher in the morning.

Al took a good, long look at the doll. Robert was dressed in a white sailor suit that looked like it was a little too big for him. The cuffs of the pants were rolled up to show off his thin, misshapen feet. He wore a sailor hat on top of his worn head. He had little black shiny

beads for eyes, and his mouth was almost nonexistent. Small holes dotted his chin and neck as if worms had burrowed into his face and left him permanently scarred.

"Is he creepy?" Selma asked, shielding her eyes.

"Not really," Al said, which was a bit of a lie.

Robert's hands, which were mostly covered by the long sleeves of the sailor shirt, looked like they'd seen better days. The fingers were a little twisted as if they'd been damaged over the many years he'd been around. Nestled in the crook of his arm was a stuffed dog with crazy bug-eyes and an open mouth. From a distance, the dog almost looked like a little lion. The two stuffed figures sat on a small wooden chair.

Once the class's murmurs settled, Corey began.

"A young boy named Robert Eugene Otto received Robert the Doll as a gift more than a hundred years ago," Corey began. "His grandfather had brought it home from Germany."

"Wait, so the boy's name was Robert too?" Charlie, who was never one to raise his hand, asked.

"At first, yes," Corey explained. "But later, he gave his beloved doll his own name and started going by his middle name instead. He liked to be called Gene."

Charlie nodded, but Al was only more skeptical. *Why would you give up your name for a doll?*

"Gene and Robert were inseparable," Corey continued. "Anywhere Gene went, Robert was right there with him. And whenever something bad happened or Gene got in trouble, he blamed it on Robert."

Robert did it, Al thought, remembering the poster near the entrance.

"What kind of stuff happened?" A girl Al couldn't see asked.

"Objects would start moving on their own. Things ended up broken, and no one could explain why," Corey said. "There were even creepier things too. Gene's family often heard a child laughing at night. They also heard footsteps in the hallway when no one else was home."

A couple of Al's classmates laughed nervously. Mrs. Crowley rubbed the outside of her arms as if she had the chills.

Is everyone actually believing these stories? Al wondered.

"Who here still carries their favorite childhood toy around with them? Anyone?" Corey asked. Al glanced at the rest of the class. No one raised their hand. "That's what I thought. When Gene was older, he still had Robert in his life. As an adult, he moved into a house and set Robert in front of a window so he could look outside."

"I'm going to have nightmares for the next three years," Selma whispered to Al.

"People would avoid walking past the house because they swore the doll was watching them. It felt like his eyes were following their every movement," Corey said. "Some even claimed to see him move."

Corey explained that when Gene died in 1974, Robert was still in the house. A new owner bought the place and put Robert in the attic, where he lived for twenty years. During that time, she reported hearing unexplained noises and movement coming from the attic.

"She finally donated Robert to the museum," Corey finished. "We weren't sure what to do with him. Word traveled that the old 'haunted' doll people used to see in Gene's window was now here at Fort East Martello. People came by asking to see it until we eventually decided to make Robert an exhibit. He's been with us ever since."

Al glanced around the rest of the room. Under a brick archway along one of the walls, there was a message in the same creepy font used on Robert's display case. It said:

Remember, you need to ask Robert's permission before you take his photo.

A bulletin board hung beneath the message. More than thirty letters were pinned to it. Some of them looked as though they were typed, while others were scrawled on torn pieces of paper.

Al was about to ask about the letters, but Mrs. Crowley beat him to it.

"Corey," she said. "Could you tell us about these messages?"

Corey smiled. "Of course," he said. "Those are letters that previous visitors have sent to Robert. They're apologies for taking his picture without permission or disrespecting him in some way."

A few gasps sounded out. Some of the students went over to look at the messages to see for themselves.

Corey continued answering questions as the class moved around Robert's case to get a better look. Al moved closer too, and could hear his classmates ask the doll if they could take his picture.

"I'm ready to get out of here," Selma said. "I'll be waiting outside."

"Are you okay?" Al asked. He knew dolls creeped Selma out, but he'd never seen her so scared. Her skin was so pale she almost looked like she was going to be sick.

"Just don't feel well," Selma said. "And Robert is making me nervous."

Without another word, she walked away to stand outside the double doors.

Al moved around the group and watched as classmate after classmate asked the doll for permission before posing next to his case. Some of them actually thanked the little sailor after getting their picture.

Are they crazy? Al thought. *It's not like the doll can speak back.* The whole thing seemed ridiculous.

"What do you think, Al?" Charlie asked. "You believe this stuff?"

Al smirked and shrugged his shoulders quickly.

"Not really," he admitted. "What about you?"

"Yeah, I didn't at first," Charlie replied. "But now, after seeing him and hearing the stories? I think there might be something to it."

"You don't think it's just an act to keep people interested?" Al asked, glancing at Robert. It almost felt like the doll was watching him, but he knew that wasn't possible.

"Could be," Charlie said. "But I'm not sure I want to find out what happens if that little guy gets mad."

"He's a doll," Al said, shaking his head. "Just an old doll some kid blamed stuff on."

"If you say so," Charlie said.

Once the rest of his class moved on to the wall of letters and other parts of the museum, Al stood in front of the museum's most popular inhabitant. He pulled his phone out of his pocket and opened up the camera.

As he did, the phone went dark as if it had suddenly lost power.

Al raised an eyebrow and looked into Robert's beady little eyes.

Nice try, pal, Al thought. *My phone's old—it does that sometimes.*

He pressed the home button to make the phone light up, then pulled up the camera once again. He held it up to capture Robert and his strange little dog. His finger hovered over the red button.

"Smile, you creepy-looking thing," Al said.

He took the picture.

As soon as he did, the camera winked out again. Al slipped the phone into his pocket without bothering to check it and walked over to the letters. Some of his classmates were reading them out loud. They remarked how spooky it was that such bad things had happened to people when they "disrespected" Robert.

Al scanned some of the letters too. People claimed they had lost money or jobs, or even ended up getting divorced, after disrespecting Robert. Some had experienced bad luck in general.

So if anything bad happens after visiting some doll in a museum, it's the doll's fault? Al wondered. *Bad things happen all the time. That's just how life goes.*

Bored of reading plea after plea for forgiveness, Al found Selma outside in the hallway, looking at an old baby carriage.

"There a doll in there?" Al asked.

"Shut up," Selma said.

"Sorry, sorry," Al replied. "You okay?"

"Yeah," she replied. "I just felt really weird in there, almost like I might throw up."

Al looked at his friend. The color had come back in her face, and she didn't look as upset as she had before. Even though he didn't get it, it seemed like Selma really had a phobia when it came to dolls. He wondered if there was a name for it.

"I took Robert's picture," Al admitted.

"You did?" Selma asked. "Well, I don't want to see it. Did you ask his permission?"

Al thought about lying to make Selma feel better but decided against it. He wanted to be honest with his friend.

"Nah," he said. "But I'm sure it'll be fine."

Almost instantly, Selma looked like she was going to be sick again.

She grabbed Al's arm. "Are you serious?"

Al smiled, hoping to calm her down. "Relax. It's all just a bunch of superstitious garbage, Selma. I don't believe in any of that stuff. Nothing bad will happen. Just watch."

Selma took a deep breath and looked him in the eye. "I hope you're right."

CHAPTER 3

BAD LOCK

"I still can't believe you did that," Selma said as she and Al boarded the bus with the rest of the class. The two of them found a seat in the middle of the bus behind Charlie and a kid named Pedro.

"It's not that big of a deal," Al said. "It's not like he came to life and started pounding on the inside of his plastic prison in anger or anything."

Selma glanced out the window as if even thinking about Robert coming to life was too much for her to take.

"But isn't it better to be safe than sorry?" Selma asked. "Just in case there's something to it?"

Al sat back in his seat as the rest of the students found places to sit. He watched as Mrs. Crowley did a quick count, mouthing the numbers to make sure she had the same number of students she'd started the day with.

"Think about how dumb that sounds," Al said, turning to his friend. "Some doll that's over a hundred years old gets mad if you don't ask his permission to take his picture. Not to mention believing the doll is alive in the first place and can think about things like being rude or—"

"Dude," Charlie said, turning around in his chair to stare at Al. "You didn't ask permission?"

"Seriously?" Al groaned. "You too?"

Charlie widened his eyes and shook his head. "You didn't get the creeps from that doll?"

"Well, sure," Al said. "The thing was definitely strange, but that's because it's old and there's a whole story made up around him. It's just the sort of thing that gets tourists to come to this place."

"I don't know," Charlie said. "The whole place felt off to me."

Al's comment had drawn Pedro's attention as well. Charlie filled him in about what Al did (or rather, didn't do), and before they were even halfway back to school, almost the entire bus knew about it.

"You're going to be cursed," Pedro told Al. "I bet Robert is mad at you for being rude and not asking to take his picture."

Al held in the urge to blow up at his superstitious classmates. He glanced around to find most of them

looking at him in horror, like he had a second nose on his face or something. They didn't even know the full story. It was one thing that he hadn't followed the rule about asking for permission. *What if they knew what I said right before I took the picture?* he wondered.

"Has everyone lost their minds?" Al asked Selma, avoiding the stares of his friends and classmates. "This is the kind of stuff we believed in when we were seven or eight. Kids think everything scary in the world is coming to get them. Heck, back then I couldn't sleep at night if my closet door was left open."

Selma shrugged. "I still can't."

"What?"

"I know, I know," Selma said and laughed. "It's weird. It has to be closed."

Just as Al was going to ask her what she thought would happen if she left the closet door open, there was a loud booming noise, and the bus began to shudder. The windows rattled in their frames, and the seats vibrated violently. The bus lurched a bit, and there was an intermittent thumping sound as the bus driver slowed down and pulled over to the side of the road.

"What did you do, Al?" Charlie cried, shaking his head.

"It's the curse," Rachel said. She covered her mouth and pointed at Al.

"It's a flat tire," the bus driver announced, leaning over to look at the side view mirror.

Al glanced at Selma, who raised her eyebrows at him as if to say, *You see?*

"Seriously? This is how it starts? Somehow Robert got out of his case, chased us down the road, and threw a handful of nails into the road to pop the tires on a busload full of students?" Al whispered. "Is that what you think?"

"No," Selma admitted. "But if he did put a curse on you, the bad luck could follow you no matter where you go. I don't really know how curses work."

"They don't," Al said. "And it stinks that anything bad that happens from now on is automatically my fault for not being polite to a dumb doll."

Selma seemed to cringe at his words.

"Think about this," she said. "How many times have you been on a school bus in your lifetime?"

"More times than I want to think about," Al admitted. "Ever since I was five, I guess."

"And has the bus ever had a flat tire in all of those times?"

"No," Al said with a smirk. He knew where she was going but decided to play along. "What about you?"

"I've been on all kinds of buses, and I've never had something like this happen," Selma said. "I bet no one here has."

"So . . ."

"So," Selma continued. "Don't you think it's a little odd that on the exact day you might've become cursed—"

"Oh, c'mon," Al shouted. "I'm not cursed!"

His outburst drew the attention of the others around him.

Selma lowered her voice so that only Al could hear. "The same day you did what you did, the bus blows a tire maybe a half hour later. What're the odds?"

"It has nothing to do with odds," Al said. "It's coincidence. Simple as that."

"Uh-huh," Selma said.

———————

It took nearly two hours for another bus to be dispatched to pick up the students stranded on the side of the A1A highway. By the time they got back to Gulf View Middle School, Al realized he was going to be late for football practice after school.

As he sprinted to the locker room, Al rounded a

corner near the gyms and smacked into Mr. Paulson, his PE teacher. Al ended up knocking the computer tablet and stainless steel coffee tumbler Mr. Paulson was carrying to the ground.

As the silver tumbler hit the wall, the cap popped off, dumping hot coffee all over the floor. The tablet took a couple of tough bounces and came to rest near a vending machine.

"Whoa, whoa," Mr. Paulson said. "Slow down, Mr. Padilla!"

Al looked at the mess he'd made and the look on his teacher's face.

"I'm sorry," he exclaimed. "We had a flat tire on the bus back from the museum and—"

"You're late for practice," Mr. Paulson said. "Coach Rieder was wondering where a chunk of his team was. He's not happy, especially after last Friday's game."

Al knew what that meant: extra laps around the football field. His coach didn't like excuses, no matter how valid they were. In his mind, his players were expected to be lined up and stretched out ten minutes before practice began.

Though he knew it was going to make him even

more late, Al crouched down to pick up the coffee tumbler. It was dented and covered with coffee.

"Oh, I totally wrecked your coffee thing," Al said. "I'm so sorry. Let me get some paper towels and—"

"Well, this old monster is shot," Mr. Paulson said, pressing the button on the side of the tablet. "It won't power up anymore."

No way, Al thought. *I completely wrecked his stuff! If I have to buy another one for him, my dad is going to lose it!*

"I am so sorry, Mr. Paulson," Al said. "It's totally my fault. Tell me what I owe you and I'll bring the money tomorrow and—"

"No, no," Mr. Paulson said, waving him off. "I've been holding out on getting a new one for a while. This will finally force me to take the plunge and buy something new."

Even though Mr. Paulson said it was fine, Al could tell he was disappointed. It was an accident that didn't need to happen, and it was all because the bus had blown a tire on the way back to school.

"I'm sorry," Al said again. "I feel terrible."

Robert did it, a creepy voice in his head said.

"That's not true," Al blurted, without even realizing he'd said the words aloud.

"Excuse me?" Mr. Paulson said.

"Sorry, I didn't mean to say that," Al said.

"Okay," Mr. Paulson said, looking at him a little strangely. "I thought you were saying it's not true that you're sorry."

"No, I'm not," Al said. "I mean, I am. I *am* sorry and I *do* feel terrible."

Mr. Paulson nodded. "Let's slow down from now on, okay?"

"For sure," Al said. "And I'll go grab some paper towels from the bathroom."

Mr. Paulson put a hand up. "Don't bother," he said. "You've got enough trouble on your plate with Coach Rieder. Get to practice and get us a win tomorrow, won't you?"

"I'll try," Al said. "Sorry again."

As Al walked away from the mess he'd made, he took a deep breath and exhaled. It was as if a chain reaction of dumb things was happening to him, starting with the incident on the bus. When he got into the locker room, he wasn't surprised to find Patrick all suited up and ready to hit the field.

"Coach is mad," Patrick said. "Thanks to you and that curse Robert put on you."

"I'm sure that's it," Al said. "Buses never break down, right?"

"Whatever, man," Patrick said. "All I know is we're doing an extra lap for every minute we're late."

"Seriously?"

"See you out there," Patrick said as he brushed past him in his shoulder pads. "And I'd hurry if I were you."

Yeah, hurrying worked so well for me last time, Al thought.

After Patrick left, Al was truly alone in the locker room. It was eerily quiet except for the occasional drip from a leaky shower faucet. Every few seconds, he could hear the watery echo as a drop plopped onto the tile floor.

Al rushed to his locker and entered the combination. The lock popped open, and he quickly got dressed, stuffed his clothes into the locker, and locked it back up. As he took a step, he realized he hadn't put his cleats on.

"Great," he muttered to himself. He grabbed the lock and spun the dial to the first number: 59. He turned it the opposite way to 7, then reversed it back to 18.

The lock didn't open.

"C'mon," he groaned.

59, 7, 18.

Nothing.

He tried again. No luck.

Al glanced at the clock and shook his head. He was officially twenty-two minutes late for practice.

He banged his fist against the locker in frustration. The sound echoed through the empty room, punctuated by another loud drip in the showers.

Through the metal meshwork on the front of the locker door, he could see his cleats inside, almost taunting him to get the door open. Taking a deep breath, Al tried again.

59, 7, 18.

Still nothing.

He tried doing the combination backward. He tried the combination for his school locker instead.

Nothing worked.

Al thought about wearing his regular shoes outside but realized he'd already locked them up, just like he always did. There was nothing for him to wear.

I can't go out there in my socks, he thought. *And every minute I stand here, the more trouble I'm in.*

Al sat down on the wooden bench that ran along the middle row of lockers. He stared at the lock, as if willing it to pop open.

Taking a deep breath, he stood up, tried the combination, and pulled.

The lock stayed locked.

Perfect, Al thought.

CHAPTER 4

NIGHT TERRORS

By the time Al got out onto the field, football practice was almost over. He had ended up finding a custodian to clip the lock for him. The custodian gave Al the ruined lock, as if it were a parting gift. Instinctively, Al tried the combination again, and the lock immediately popped open.

"How 'bout that," the custodian said.

Great, Al thought. *All of that for nothing. And now I need to get a new lock.*

Fully suited up, Al hit the field to find Coach Rieder less than happy to see him.

"Coach, it's been a tough day," Al admitted.

"And it's going to be tougher when you're on the bench tomorrow night," his coach fired back. "Start running, Padilla."

Mercifully, his coach let him off the hook after ten laps around the field. Even so, Al was completely exhausted by the time he got home. He wanted nothing more than to eat something quick and collapse into bed.

As he walked in the back door, his dad was already on him.

"Eat something quick and then—"

"Bed," Al said.

"Paper," his dad reminded him.

"I'm so exhausted, Dad," Al groaned, flopping down into a chair at the kitchen table. There was a plate of ropa vieja waiting for him.

"It's due tomorrow, no?"

Al poked his fork into the shredded beef and yellow rice. With a long exhale, he nodded. He *had* to turn in his paper tomorrow, especially since it was game day. His grades had already taken a bit of a hit since joining the team. The worst thing he could do was turn in a terrible, late paper.

Even with his dad hovering over him while he was eating, Al managed to wolf down most of his meal, leaving only a few olives and a shriveled pepper on his plate.

"How was the museum today?" Dad asked.

Al wanted to laugh, but he was too sore to move. "Mostly terrible," he said. "Saw a bunch of old stuff, including that haunted doll."

"And?"

"Kind of a joke," Al admitted and instantly felt a

small ringing in his ears. He shook it off. "Pretty much everyone in my class fell for it. They were all creeped out by the thing."

Dad took his plate and rinsed it in the sink.

"Every place needs a trick or a gimmick to stay in business, Alejandro," Dad said. "Guess theirs is a spooky doll."

"Surprised you didn't get a souvenir," Marco teased from the dining room.

I went to the Fort East Martello Museum, and all I got was a lousy curse from an ugly doll, Al thought. *Not that I believe it for a second.*

"It was between the Robert T-shirt, a bottle opener, and a set of decorative coasters," Al joked. "I just couldn't decide."

"Paper, paper, paper," Dad said, clapping his hands together with each *paper.* "Now. Go."

"Fine," Al said, standing up with a groan. His legs were worn out, and he knew he was going to be in even worse shape in the morning.

———

Al sat at the desk in his bedroom upstairs to work on his paper. After looking up a few websites on weather and plugging a few extra facts into his report, he opened a new browser window.

Don't do it, he told himself.

Fighting the urge, Al went back to his report and reread it out loud. Any time he stumbled across some clumsy wording, he fixed it and started reading from that paragraph again. He spent about twenty minutes fine-tuning the report, then struck the keyboard shortcut to save his work.

As soon as his finger hit the S key, the computer winked out, turning the screen black.

"No," Al whispered.

Feeling his heart start to thrum inside his chest, Al pressed the power button to restart his computer. The computer logo illuminated the screen, followed by a warning shaming him for not shutting down his PC correctly. According to the warning, he might have damaged his hard drive.

"Not my fault," Al said to the screen before hitting ENTER to continue.

Robert did it, a childlike voice whispered in his head.

"Shut up," Al said. "That's ridiculous."

Once his computer was up and running, Al hurriedly

went to his file folders and looked for his report. His heart sank as he scrolled through the files.

It wasn't there. Not even the rough draft he'd opened after dinner.

"No way," he gasped. "No, no, no way."

Al backed up and did a search for his report's file name. He watched in anticipation as the progress bar moved at a sloth speed. When it was finally done, it gave him the news he was dreading:

NO FILE FOUND.

It was gone. The report was gone, even what he'd worked on over the past two weeks. All of the great info he'd dug up about the Civil War was completely gone.

Al wanted to cry.

He looked at the alarm clock next to his bed with exhausted eyes. The red digital letters told him it was 9:43 p.m.

"I'm in trouble," Al said to his computer screen. He knew that if a whole system search didn't turn it up, there was no way he was going to find it.

He sat in the silence of his room, thinking about what it would take to rewrite the entire paper before tomorrow morning. As he did, he felt a cold chill run up his spine. It felt as if an air conditioner vent was pumping a chilly gust directly onto his back.

A loud knock at the door made him nearly jump out of his chair.

"How's the paper?" His dad asked from the hallway.

Terrible, Al thought and opened up a new file to start fresh.

It was a little after one in the morning when Al finally printed off his new report. He slipped it into his folder and put the folder into his backpack. As a precaution, he e-mailed the report to himself and saved it in three different places on his computer. Even if his computer gave out, the paper would still exist somewhere.

"Nice try, Robert," Al said. *What are you saying?* He thought. He must have been going delirious from exhaustion.

He stepped into the hallway to make his way to the bathroom to get ready for bed. As expected, the rest of the house was silent. Al quickly brushed his teeth and headed back to his room. He dropped onto his unmade bed and crawled to his pillows for his sleepy salvation.

In a matter of minutes, Al was asleep.

He dreamed of running what felt like an endless

distance down the football field in his socks. As he looked down, he could see that his feet were muddy and grass-stained. The ends of the socks were loose and floppy, slapping against his legs as he ran. Al turned to see a small figure sitting in the otherwise empty stands.

With his next step, Al fell to the ground, sliding along the wet, dewy grass.

Somewhere, he heard what sounded like a small child giggling.

Al awoke with a start, his ears ringing as the adrenaline racing through his veins made a circuit through his body.

Who was that?

Al glanced at the clock on his bedside table to see that it was 2:12 a.m. He'd been asleep for barely an hour.

He lay his head back on his pillow and listened. The ringing in his ears subsided, though his heart still thumped wildly in his chest. He waited to see if he could hear the laughter again.

Was the laughing just in my dream, or did I actually hear it? Al wondered. *Something must have woken me up . . .*

Though he knew there was nothing there, he turned the lamp on. The light illuminated his desk, video game posters, and bookshelf. Nothing seemed out of the ordinary. He even glanced at his computer, half expecting to see some cruel doll trying to erase his new report.

There was nothing there.

Satisfied that he had merely dreamt the noise, Al turned off the lamp, mashed his head back into the pillow, and closed his eyes. He knew that he wouldn't return to the dream of him running in his socks. Dreams didn't work that way. He tried to think about something else to calm himself down.

He took a few deep breaths and let his tired mind take over.

Then Al heard the laughing again, followed by footsteps. The sounds seemed to be coming from the hallway.

Al sat straight up in his bed, his heart going into triple overdrive. Someone was messing with him. That had to be it.

"Marco?" Al called. "Dude, it isn't funny, man."

Al climbed out of bed and turned his lamp on for extra precaution. Strange shadows danced along the walls before he realized they were his own. He carefully walked to his bedroom door and cracked it open.

"Marco?" he called. If some childlike voice responded with "Polo," he was going to scream.

Thankfully, there was no answer.

Al opened his door, cringing as it creaked on its hinges. He stepped into the hallway and walked past the dark bathroom. He sucked in his breath, almost certain something was going to grab him from the darkness and pull him inside.

He let the air out of his lungs when that didn't happen.

Al approached Marco's open bedroom door and peered in. His older brother was sprawled out on his back, his mouth open. He was fast asleep.

Further into the house, he heard the squeak the stairs made leading down to the main floor.

Someone is in the house, Al thought. *Or some*thing.

To ensure it wasn't his dad, Al continued on to the end of the hallway to his dad's bedroom. The telltale sound of his dad's deep, rhythmic snoring told him that he, too, was sound asleep.

It's Robert, the childlike voice in his head said. *Robert did it.*

"Not possible," Al whispered into the dark, mostly to reassure himself. He knew that if he got on his bike, rode to the museum, and got inside, he'd find the battered old sailor doll in its case, just as they'd left it the day before. Dolls don't just get up and walk around.

You didn't ask his permission, the voice said. *You made him mad.*

"Get it together, Al," he told himself. "You don't believe in this stuff. No one over the age of nine should believe in this stuff. It's just touristy nonsense."

Al continued to the stairs and carefully made his way to the first level, turning lights on as he went. After reaching the final step, he turned to walk into the living room. The room was as silent and dark as it should be at that time in the morning.

Al heard the sound of a car approaching on the street. As the headlights passed their house, a shadow outside was revealed near the front window. It looked like a skinny, childlike figure, watching him from about ten feet away.

"Oh no," Al whispered.

As the car passed, it looked like the figure was moving closer to him as if waiting for its moment to strike. Soon, the room was once again shrouded in darkness. As Al passed through the living room doorway, he felt something touch him on the small of his back. He swore it felt like a hand.

Al screamed.

CHAPTER 5

SEEING RED

"Alejandro!" a familiar voice said. "What's the matter? What are you doing at this hour?"

Al turned around to see the sleepy face of his dad, partially lit from the light in the stairway. His breath rushed out of him like a balloon releasing all of its air in one sputtering gust.

"You scared me," Al said, almost breathlessly. He put his hand to his chest as if to calm his heart. "I thought you were something else."

His dad gave him a puzzled look.

"I thought something was wrong," his dad said, pointing to the lights Al had turned on along the stairs. "Why are you up so early? You've got school tomorrow, rememb—"

"I know, I know," Al said. "I just thought I heard something. Footsteps or a voice."

"It's that doll," his dad said. "Marco got it in your head, and now you're having nightmares."

Not you too, Al thought.

"I'm not having nightmares, Dad," Al said, which wasn't completely true. He had seen some strange little figure in his football field dream. "I think I'm just worn out. Long day, that's all."

His dad clapped him on the shoulder. "Get some sleep," he said. "The big game is tomorrow night."

Yeah, Al thought. *About that. Sounds like I'm going to be benched.*

"Okay," Al said. "Good night, Dad."

His dad yawned and gave him a wave before plodding back upstairs.

"And turn off these lights," his dad said once he was in the upstairs hallway.

"I will," Al promised.

When he heard his dad's footsteps in the bedroom above him, Al turned the light on in the living room. He glanced at the front window where he'd sworn he'd seen the shadow. There was nothing there. Feeling a little brave, he advanced to the thin curtain and reached his hand out to pull it open.

If there's a face staring in at me, I'm going to scream again, Al thought. He closed his eyes and tugged the curtain to the side. Hearing nothing but his heart beating rapidly, he squinted through his shuttered eyelids.

Just outside the front window was the small shrub that was always there.

It was just a shadow from the car that passed by, Al thought. *It's not that doll. It never was.*

Taking one last glance out into the dark, Al closed the curtain. He shut off the light in the living room and all the other lights until he was back in bed. Once he was nestled into his pillow again, he closed his heavy eyes and tried to fall asleep.

"Tomorrow is going to be much easier than today," he whispered to himself.

There's no way it could get any worse, he thought. And with that in his head, he fell asleep.

———————

A beam of sunlight struck Al in the face, and he woke up with a start. He rolled over to look at his alarm clock, only to find it was completely dark.

"No," he groaned and sat up. Crawling up against the wall, he peered behind his nightstand to find the plug pulled from the socket.

Impossible, he thought. He recalled seeing the time on the clock a couple times the night before, both when he'd lost his report and when he'd woken up to the sound of . . . something in his house.

Now it's unplugged.

He grabbed his phone off his desk to see what time it was.

8:02 a.m.

Remembering his report, he quickly opened his bag and checked his folder. Thankfully, it was still there, and all of the pages had words on them. The way his luck had gone over the past twelve hours, he knew it was in his best interest to double check.

"I'm going to be late," he murmured.

He ran downstairs, buttoning his shorts and pulling on a clean T-shirt. His brother was just heading out the door.

"Marco," Al called. "Wait!"

"Did you oversleep?" Marco asked, looking hurried. "I thought you'd already left for school, otherwise I would've woken you up!"

"Did you unplug my clock?"

Marco looked at his younger brother like he'd fallen out of the sky. "Why would I do that?"

"To mess with me," Al said. "Make me think I'm cursed or something."

"Yeah, okay, bro," Marco said. "I need to go. Good luck getting to school on time."

Before Al could say anything more, Marco was gone.

When Al and Marco had gone to the same school, they could travel there together. But since Marco was now in high school, his start time was different, leaving his younger brother to fend for himself.

Grabbing his backpack and a cold toaster pastry to eat on the way, Al ran out the door and headed for school.

———————

Al ran into Selma right before their US history class. As he'd done countless times before, he checked his folder to ensure his report was where it was supposed to be.

It was.

"You okay?" Selma asked as they walked down the hall together.

"Besides being late for school and getting maybe five hours of sleep?" Al replied. "Yeah, I'm great."

He filled her in on everything that had happened since he'd last seen her on the bus back from the museum. As he did, she shook her head slightly. Al wasn't sure if that meant she didn't believe him, or something else entirely.

"I told you," she said.

"You're kidding, right?" Al replied.

"It's all happening because of what you did," Selma said. "Do you believe it now?"

"No," Al said. "I don't believe it. The stuff with practice happened because the bus had gotten a flat tire."

"Even your locker not opening for you?" Selma asked. "That was because of the bus too?"

"Sure," Al said as he found a seat toward the back of the class. "I was in a hurry so I messed up the combination. It happens all the time."

"You've had janitors cut locks open for you *all the time?*"

"No," Al mumbled under his breath. "You know what I mean. I was frazzled because I was late."

"Uh-huh," Selma said and gave him a thumbs up. It was her way of saying: *Whatever you say, Al.*

Mrs. Crowley came into the classroom and closed the door behind her. She was an older lady who wore her long gray hair piled into a bun on the top of her head. Al always thought it looked like a cinnamon roll.

"Happy Friday," she said as she walked in front of the classroom. "Glad to see all of your shining faces this morning. But I have to say, some of them look a little more tired than others."

Great, Al thought. *She's talking about me.*

"Before we jump into our next section, let's take care of business first," Mrs. Crowley said. "I believe there might be reports coming my way, yes?"

All around Al, everyone opened their binders and rifled through their folders. The students passed their reports to the end of each table. Before Al passed his up, he flipped through the pages and nearly screamed at what he saw.

Across each of the four pages and scrawled in red crayon were the words *YOU WEREN'T NICE TO ME.*

Every. Single. Page.

"This can't be happening," Al whispered. He flipped back and forth to each of the pages. Someone must have gotten into his locker and messed with his report.

"Is there a problem, Mr. Padilla?" Mrs. Crowley asked, heading down the aisle toward him. "You look upset."

His ears burned in embarrassment as he felt the eyes of all twenty-one of his classmates staring at him. He kept looking at the pages, expecting them to change somehow, but they didn't. His report was ruined.

"Who did this?" Al asked, standing up from his chair. "Which one of you did this to my report?"

He glanced around at everyone else in the classroom. Everyone, including Selma, looked back at him like they were completely confused.

"Alejandro," Mrs. Crowley said calmly. "What's happened?"

Al ignored his teacher as she came closer to him. He held his report up in his hand and turned, expecting to see one of his classmates laughing behind their hands at the prank they'd pulled on him.

"How did you get into my locker?" Al demanded, looking around wild-eyed. "How did you know my combination?"

"Al," Selma whispered. "Stop it."

"Alejandro," Mrs. Crowley said. "I need you to lower your voice, please."

Al felt his eyes grow hot in anger. He knew someone had done this to him, and he wanted to find out who.

"They've wrecked my report," Al said. "Someone here is trying to make me believe in that doll curse, but I know it's all fake. None of that stuff is real!"

Mrs. Crowley put her hand on Al's arm.

"Can I see the report?" she asked gently. "Let me see what happened."

Al shook his head. He didn't want to give it to her. He was pretty sure that if he did, she'd automatically draw an F across the front page.

"Please," Mrs. Crowley asked. "It's all right."

Reluctantly, Al handed the paper he'd rebuilt from scratch to his history teacher. She took it carefully from him and flipped through the pages.

"Well," Mrs. Crowley said.

"They ruined it," Al said. "They wrote on all the pages."

"Can you show me where?" Mrs. Crowley asked. "I don't see what you mean."

Al pulled his stare away from his awe-struck class-mates and looked to his teacher.

"It's on all of them," Al said. "You can't miss it."

Mrs. Crowley held the report out to Al and flipped through the pages. There wasn't a single mark. The report was just as he'd left it when he'd finished it early that morning.

"There was . . . " Al muttered. "It was written in crayon. Red crayon."

Mrs. Crowley closed the paper and put it with the others under her arm.

"It looks good to me," she said and smiled. "Nicely done."

I don't get it, Al thought. *I saw it with my own eyes. It was right there!*

"Are you feeling okay?" Mrs. Crowley asked. "Perhaps you should stop in at the nurse's office. You look really pale."

Al nodded. He didn't feel sick—just disoriented and embarrassed that he'd made a complete fool of himself. His classmates were looking at him funny too.

"I'll go," Al whispered and grabbed his binder.

No one spoke as he walked out of the classroom and into the hallway.

The hallways were silent as Al walked past Mr. Prust's math class and the janitor's closet. It almost felt as if school had been canceled—he was the only one in sight. There was no sound coming from the other classrooms, making him feel like either everyone was taking a test or they'd heard about his outburst and were afraid to say something.

Farther down the hallway was the main office, which held the nurse's office inside. Al's footsteps seemed extra loud, nearly echoing down the long, empty hallways.

Behind him, Al heard a creak.

He turned to see the janitor's closet door open slightly, revealing a sliver of darkness between the door and the doorframe. If someone was in there, they were standing in the pitch dark.

"Hello?" Al asked before he realized what he was doing.

He knew that if someone were playing a prank on him, they would be loving how scared and freaked out he probably looked.

Al stood for a moment, watching the door. As he did, he saw a small white face peer out at him from inside the closet. The face had black, beady eyes that didn't

blink. They just stared. Al backed away, moving closer to the main office.

He turned to see where he was going, then glanced back over his shoulder. When he looked at the closet again, Al saw the door was closed.

CHAPTER 6

LUNCH BREAKDOWN

"What happened to you?"

Selma was sitting at their usual spot in the lunchroom, leaving a space for Al. As he slumped down across from her, he let out a huge sigh. He felt like everyone in the lunchroom was watching him, even though they weren't.

"I must just be sleep deprived," Al said. "Staying up that late and with everything that happened yesterday? It got the better of me."

"You totally freaked out in Mrs. Crowley's class," Selma said. "I've never seen you like that."

"I know," Al admitted. "I made a complete fool out of myself."

He poked his fork into his pile of spaghetti and spread the sauce around. Moving a meatball out of the way, he twirled a bite around the metal tongs.

"Did you really see something on your paper?"

Al glanced at the others around them. No one seemed to be listening in, but he still wanted to be careful.

"I did," Al said. "Or at least I thought I did."

Selma bit into her sandwich and chewed it slowly before taking a sip from her water bottle.

"What did it say?"

Al managed a fake laugh that felt foreign coming out of his mouth. Nothing that had happened to him in the past day was funny, but he wanted to make it seem like nothing was bothering him.

"You're going to laugh," he said as if to warn her.

"I doubt it," Selma said. "But tell me anyway."

Here goes, Al thought. "Okay, so it looked like the words *YOU WEREN'T NICE TO ME* were written on each of the four pages of my report," Al blurted. "It was like a little kid wrote it. The letters were all written kind of messy."

"You weren't nice to me?" Selma repeated. "Who weren't you nice to? Robert?"

Al shrugged. "I guess that's what I was supposed to believe."

Selma held a chip in her fingers and turned it over

a few times, like she was thinking really hard. "But the writing wasn't there after all."

"Nope," Al said. "So, it just means my mind is playing tricks on me."

"How were you not nice?" Selma asked, as if not wanting to let it go. "Because you didn't ask Robert's permission before taking his photo?"

The words Al said at the Fort East Martello Museum replayed in his head as if from a recording.

Smile, you creepy-looking thing.

"I might've said something not so nice," Al admitted. "Right before I took the picture."

Selma dropped her chip onto the lunchroom table.

"What did you say?" Selma whispered.

Al poked at his spaghetti a little more. Suddenly, he wasn't very hungry, but he knew he should eat. He also knew Selma was waiting to hear what he'd said.

"I might've called the doll creepy looking," Al said slowly.

Selma leaned forward and rested her elbows on the table. She cradled her temples with her fingers as if the new information had given her an instant headache.

"You're kidding me, right?" Selma said. "You not

only broke the one rule they gave you, but you threw an insult on top of it?"

The way Selma looked at him, Al felt like he'd taken a big bite from an idiot sandwich.

"Yeah," he said. "I guess I did."

Selma threw the rest of her uneaten lunch into her bag.

"It's a doll, Selma," Al said, sensing she was angry with him. "I wanted to prove that the whole curse thing was just a far-fetched lie!"

Some of the other students at the table began glancing at them.

"Yeah?" Selma said, turning to look at Al. "And how's that going for you, so far?"

Al thought about all the bad luck he'd had in the past day.

"People have bad days," Al said. "I refuse to believe that some old dead-eyed doll sitting on display in a museum is making all these awful things happen to me. It's just coincidence. Or maybe people are messing with me, thinking it's funny."

Selma folded her arms and gave him a dirty look.

"So, someone here at school is making you see words that aren't really there?"

"No," Al said. "Don't be ridiculous. That's just because I'm exhausted and I've got this dumb doll on my mind."

"Yeah, keep insulting him," Selma said. "So what did the nurse say?"

"He said I'm probably dehydrated and short on sleep," Al said. "I drank a bottle of water and took a little nap. I'm fine, now. Really."

Selma shook her head. "I'm not so sure about that."

"Nothing else is going to happen," Al said. "Making a scene in Mrs. Crowley's class was probably the last of it."

Al thought about the stuff he didn't tell Selma, like the face he'd seen in the janitor's closet or even the noises he'd heard the night before. Considering his friend was already scared of dolls, he thought it best to leave some of the creepier stuff he'd imagined out of the conversation.

"I think you know what you need to do," Selma said, standing up from her spot at the table.

"What's that?" Al asked.

"Write a letter to Robert," she said. "Beg for his forgiveness."

And end up on the "wall of shame" with all of the

other dummies who believe in this supernatural garbage? Al thought. *No way!*

"Think about how dumb that sounds," Al said. "It's a doll, Selma. It can't read any more than it can do half the things people think it can do."

Selma sighed and rubbed her eyes.

"I think it's going to get worse before it gets better," she said.

Al shrugged. "It's fine," he said. "Really. Everything is going to be fine. Things will turn around, and everyone will forget about Robert's so-called curse. You'll see."

"I hope so," Selma said, then looked across the lunchroom. "I'll see you a little later, okay?"

"Yeah," Al said. "Sounds good."

He felt a little hurt and confused. They usually hung out for the duration of lunch, but Selma almost seemed anxious to get away from him. Al watched her walk to the garbage can, pitch her mostly uneaten lunch, and head for the door.

Knowing he had a game later on, Al got to work eating the rest of his lukewarm spaghetti. The coach had told him he was going to be on the bench for the game, but he knew that could change.

He stuck a huge helping of saucy pasta into his

mouth and used the edge of his fork to cut into a meat-ball. As he did, he heard a sickening crunch.

A bone? Al wondered.

It was much, much worse.

He moved his fork away and looked down at the split meatball. There were little black shapes inside. Upon closer inspection, Al could see the shapes had little sharp legs and shells.

Beetles.

Al dropped his fork and jumped back from the table like he'd been electrocuted. He watched his plate carefully, expecting to see the little creatures scurry across his food and away from his hot lunch tray.

None of them moved.

"What the heck!?" Al cried out.

"You okay, Al?" Rachel asked. She glanced at her friends nearby, then back at him, her eyebrows raised in concern.

"That's sick," Al stammered, pointing at his plate. "Did you see that?"

Audrey and a few of the other students nearby looked over at his tray. None of them seemed as disgusted by the dead beetles in his meatball as Al did.

"I always bring something from home," Pedro admitted, holding up a peanut butter and jelly sandwich. "I've never liked the hot lunches here."

"Don't eat the meatballs, then," Audrey offered. "Pretty simple, really."

Al looked at his classmates in disbelief. Did they actually think a bunch of dead bugs in a meatball was okay? That he should just eat around it?

"There are bugs in there," Al said, pointing. "Tell me you guys aren't seeing this."

Everyone at the table leaned forward to take a look. Rodrigo got up and stood next to Al to see it from where he was standing.

"Just looks like a mushy meatball to me, bro," Rodrigo said.

Al blinked, letting his eyes close for more than a second. When he opened them again, he looked down at his plate.

There were no beetles. In their place was a meatball, split in half, looking exactly the way it should. Al even grabbed the fork to poke around at it a bit, half expecting to see a shelled bug run for cover inside what remained of his noodles.

Nothing.

"You doing okay, Al?" Rodrigo asked.

He put his hand on Al's shoulder but looked back at the others. Al could see Rodrigo make a mock scared face at the rest of the lunch table as if to say, *I'm almost scared to be close to this guy!*

"I'm fine," Al said. "I will be, anyway."

Someone at the table laughed, but Al ignored her. Shaking Rodrigo's hand from his shoulder, he dropped his fork back onto his tray and snatched it up. He took it to the garbage can and tipped the remainder of his lunch into the trash.

He returned the tray to the dirty bin then took a few deep breaths and rubbed his tired eyes.

Being this tired is making me see things, he thought. *Ruined papers, faces in the custodian's closet, and now bugs in my lunch.*

He glanced over his shoulder to see the entire table of students staring back at him, as if they expected him to do something else ridiculous. Shaking his head, Al walked out of the lunchroom and into the hallway to his locker. There were still a few minutes before lunch was over, but he knew he didn't want to sit with people who thought he was losing his mind.

Al put his hand on the lock and paused for a moment. He thought about the day before in the football locker room and the trouble he'd had. With a smile, he spun the combination and pulled up on the silver latch to open the door.

It didn't open.

Not again, Al thought and tried the combination again.

He kept his finger on the latch and closed his eyes to concentrate.

You're tired and having a bad day, Al thought. *Take your time and open your locker already.*

With a sharp, upward tug, Al felt the latch slide up, just as it had pretty much every other time so far. With a click and a squeak of metal, his locker opened.

As the small, metal door swung wide, a hand reached out to grab him.

Al shouted and fell backward, tripping over his own feet. He landed hard on his butt, sending a dull pain through his legs. It felt like the wind had been knocked out of him.

It followed me here, his mind screamed. *That rotten old doll actually came after me!*

He closed his eyes and scrambled backward until his back struck the bank of lockers on the opposite side of the hall. There was nothing Al wanted to do more than run down the hallway, out the exit, and toward home.

Was it even safe there?

In his mind, Al saw the plain, wooden face of Robert the Doll. The expressionless features of the antique sailor made him shiver.

"Leave me alone!" Al shouted.

CHAPTER 7

GAME ON

Feeling like his heart might burst inside his body, Al looked up. There, dangling outside his open locker door was the sleeve to his sweatshirt. He could see the rest of his stuff inside, including a few notebooks and a bottle with water in it from a few weeks ago.

There wasn't an angry antique doll in his locker.

"Dude," a voice called from his left.

Al turned to see a dark blue jersey with a large white number 31 across the chest. *Patrick.*

"You okay, man?" Patrick stood over Al and extended a hand to help him up.

"I don't know," Al admitted, then changed his mind. "I mean, yeah. I'm fine."

"Kind of freaked me out there for a second," Patrick said. He nodded over at the opposite wall. "You in some kind of a fight with your locker or something?"

"Very funny," Al said and forced himself to smile. "I'm just tired, and something startled me, that's all. I think I'm seeing things from lack of sleep."

"Whoa," Patrick said, taking a step away from Al. "You're supposed to be wearing your jersey. It's game day, man!"

Al nodded. In his rush to get out the door that morning, he'd completely forgotten to wear his home jersey.

"Is this because you're sitting tonight?" Patrick asked. "I mean, I know you're mad, but c'mon. We're still a team, Padilla."

"No, no. It's not that," Al promised. "I completely forgot. It's probably best I'm not playing tonight anyway. I'm not having a great day."

"Probably that curse," Patrick said. "Everyone's saying so."

Great, Al thought. *Word's still getting around.*

"Well, thanks for the hand," Al said. "I'll see you tonight, I guess."

Patrick saluted Al before turning and heading down the hall.

"And hey, Padilla?" Patrick called over his shoulder. "Maybe think about leaving that bad luck at home tonight, okay?"

The crowd erupted into applause as Alejandro Padilla and the rest of the Gulf View Giants ran onto the field later that night. They'd gotten a big pep talk from Coach Rieder, who told them that last week's loss didn't matter.

"All that matters is tonight," Al said, repeating the chant they'd all said only minutes before.

He scanned the bleachers to see if he could find his dad and brother. There were more people than he expected in the crowd, making it nearly impossible to pick them out. They'd been pretty good at showing up to his games. Marco even made a point to not be scheduled at the grocery store so he could see his little brother play.

"I think there's a lot of people from Holy Trinity in our bleachers," said Jake, their quarterback. "The visitor side bleachers are full, so they're clogging up ours."

"Well, that just means we need to send them home with tears in their eyes," Patrick said, clapping both Jake and Al on their shoulder pads. "Let's go, boys!"

Al smiled and grabbed Patrick by the jersey, head-butting his teammate with his helmet. Their team-mates also gathered around, riling themselves up for the big game. Despite the way his day had gone, Al felt good for the first time in what felt like forever. He'd gotten in a quick nap at home and ate a decent dinner before the game. Even though he knew he wasn't going to be playing much, he was happy to have his mind occupied with something other than a doll.

Al was in such a good mood he didn't even notice the shift in the weather. Gray clouds rolled in from the horizon, almost undetectable above the bright field lights at Gulf View Field.

———————

It was just after halftime when the rain started to fall. There wasn't much at first, but in typical Florida fashion, it grew steadier as the night went on. Coach Rieder brought the offensive lineup in during the turnover and gathered them around. Al stood up from the bench and went over to listen.

"It's just a little rain, boys," Coach Rieder said. "Don't let this slip away from us. We've got them by nine points and they're tired and in our house, right?"

The team shouted a jumble of *yeahs* and *rights* to show their coach they were still in the game. Al joined in too. Part of him hoped Coach would put him on the line so he could redeem himself for missing the bulk of practice the day before.

"How's the ankle, Rogers?" Coach Rieder asked Lionel, their right tackle.

"A little tight, but I'm okay," Lionel replied. He lifted his foot up and twisted his muddy cleat as if to show him he could still move it.

"Let's give it a break," Coach Rieder told him, looking at his clipboard and then at the rest of the players gathered around him. He caught Al's eye, but then moved along the line of tired faces before coming back to him.

"Padilla," the coach said. "Let's get you in there a bit. Think we can put you to work?"

"For sure," Al said, snapping his chin strap to show he meant business.

Coach Rieder smacked the top of Al's helmet with his clipboard and nodded, chomping his gum like it had done him wrong. As the coach stood up and turned to the field, Al watched Patrick pick off a sloppy downfield pass.

"Interception by number 31," the announcer boomed over the loudspeaker. "Patrick McGovern!"

A moment later, a swarm of Trinity's Tigers tackled Patrick near the 40-yard line.

"Time to bury them, guys!" Jake shouted, leading his team onto the rain-drenched field. "Let's go!"

The Giants' offensive squad hit the field and got into position on the 43-yard line. Al glanced up at the scoreboard on the far end of the field. The rain was coming down even harder now, making everything seem a little blurry. Even so, he managed to make out the score:

GIANTS: 15

VISITOR: 6

What a lucky break, Al thought as Jake started the play. *Things are finally starting to turn around. Now to make Coach glad he put me in.*

The ball was snapped, and the Tigers' defensive line surged forward. Al planted his feet as the defensive end tried to move around the outside. As soon as Al laid his shoulder into his opponent, a bright flash appeared from above. A large boom of thunder split the sky, and a bolt of light slashed down onto Gulf View Field.

There was an explosion of sparks as the scoreboard was struck by lightning. The digital score and the game clock blinked twice and then blacked out completely. A moment later, the entire field went dark as the overhead lights shut off.

Cries sounded from the bleachers as rain continued to fall and thunder rumbled overhead. Al felt temporarily blinded as his eyes adjusted from the bright flash to complete darkness. He could hear his teammates scrambling to find their way back to the sidelines. Small

lights lit up the stands as people used their cell phones to illuminate the confused crowd.

Al squinted in the dark and saw dark blue jerseys and semi-illuminated numbers move toward the Giants bench. He blinked and opened his eyes, watching them slowly adjust.

"Did you do this, Padilla?" Patrick asked from behind. "This part of your doll curse? More bad luck?"

"Yeah," Al said. "That's it. A doll has the ability to

control weather and ruin football games. That makes a whole lot of sense."

How stupid can you be? Al thought.

"I don't know," Patrick said. "A whole lot of weird stuff happens when you're around. I'm almost afraid to be near you, man."

"Then get away from me," Al said, feeling his anger rise. "Problem solved."

Coach Rieder gathered the team together and led them to the equipment garage. A handful of parents stood around their huddle with their flashlight apps on. It wasn't much light, but Al could see his coach's face and most of the rest of his team. Some of them gave him dirty looks, making him realize that Patrick wasn't the only one who thought he was a bad luck charm.

"We're going to stay inside here until the storm blows over," his coach said. He looked out the garage door to check the sky. "I haven't seen any flashes since the big one, but we need to keep you guys safe. Once we get the all-clear, we'll see if we can restore the power and finish this game."

Coach Rieder zipped up his windbreaker.

"What about the Tigers?" Jake asked. "Are they stuck out in the storm?"

"Nah," Owen replied. "They all ran to their bus."

"I'll be right back, boys," Coach Rieder said. "Stay here." Before anyone could respond, he dashed across the wet pavement toward a couple men standing near the bleachers.

Outside, the sky continued to rumble as the Gulf View Giants stood huddled together, soaking wet. Al unsnapped his helmet and took it off.

"Might want to keep that on, Al," Owen, one of their running backs, joked. "The way your day is going, this whole garage might come down."

"If that's what it takes for you to shut up, I'm all for it," Al replied.

A chorus of *oooohs* broke out among the players.

"Big talk from a guy who's scared of his own locker," Owen returned.

Al turned to look at Patrick, who had been the only one from the team to see him freak out earlier.

Thanks, Pat, Al thought. *You're a heck of a guy telling everyone about that.*

Al kept quiet, watching the storm. He could see the game's spectators head for their cars to wait it out. The parking lot was lit up with headlights as the rain continued to fall. Rumbles of thunder made the metal siding on the garage rattle and vibrate.

"This stinks," Jake said. "We were actually winning for once."

The team was silent as the rain continued to fall, and the sky grumbled and coughed.

"There's no way we're going to keep playing tonight," Lionel said. "Game over, guys."

A few minutes later, Coach Rieder ran back across the rain-slicked pavement toward the garage. He held his clipboard over his head to keep the rain off his already sodden hat.

"That's game, gentlemen," the coach said, wiping the moisture off the end of his nose. "They said they can't work on the electrical until tomorrow morning, anyway, so we're calling it. We'll be playing a Saturday game sometime soon to finish what we started."

There were rumbles among the players.

"Will we start with the same score?" Jake asked.

"I'm not sure how that will work, to be honest," the coach said. "We'll have to talk about it with the officials. It doesn't look like there's any more lightning, so I want you to get home and dry off. We don't need the whole team getting sick from being out in the rain all night."

Al thought going home sounded like a good idea. It had been a long day.

"All right, bring it in, guys," Coach Rieder said, putting his hand out. Everyone else followed suit.

"1, 2, 3," Jake began.

"STOMP, STOMP, STOMP, GIANTS!" the Gulf View Giants shouted.

With that, the team dispersed, running down the wet pavement that lined the football field to the parking lot closer to the school. Al jogged behind them, trying to figure out which set of headlights in the parking lot were his dad's.

As he got closer, Al still couldn't find them.

Didn't they make it to the game?

As his teammates jumped into their parents' cars and drove off into the night, there were only a few cars left. One of them was Coach Rieder's.

"Great," Al muttered, wiping rain from his eyes.

Behind him he could hear the crackle of gravel underneath a shoe.

He turned around to see a small shadow walking along the path toward him.

Al backed up, his cleats squelching in the mud with each step. He pulled out his phone and dialed his brother's number. He put the phone to his ear, never taking his eye off the path and what was coming his way.

The sky above him flickered with lightning, lighting up the school grounds for a split second. And in that flash, Al saw the blank, expressionless face of Robert the Doll.

CHAPTER 8

PHOTO FRENZY

This can't be real! Al thought.

He backed up from the grass, keeping his eyes on the darkened path. With the light leaving a colored stain on his eyes, Al couldn't see a thing. He had no idea if Robert was still coming or running after him. The heels of his cleats struck a cement parking barrier and he fell backward, landing in an empty parking space and splashing down into a puddle.

Water soaked his gray football pants, making them even heavier than they already were. His hands scrabbled across the gravely surface as he tried to push himself back up onto his feet.

He could hear a faint voice coming from somewhere in the dark.

"Hello? Al?"

Robert knows my name! Al's mind screamed. The voice sounded tiny and very far away.

He turned and realized he was still holding his rain-spattered phone.

The screen on his phone showed a face. A familiar one.

His brother's.

"Marco?" Al asked, bringing the phone back to his ear. "Is that you?"

"Yeah, bro," Marco said. "Where the heck are you?"

Al climbed to his feet, still watching the path where he'd seen the doll's face. In all the commotion, he couldn't hear the doll's footsteps anymore, which made him even more frightened.

Was it waiting to pounce on me? Finish the job?

"I'm in the parking lot," Al cried. "You guys didn't come to the game, so I'm stuck out here all alone!"

"Dude," Marco said. "We're at the end of the lot. Everyone else came and got in their cars. We've been waiting for you."

As much as it terrified Al to take his gaze away from the pathway, he turned. There, in the corner of the lot was his dad's car. Whoever was behind the wheel clicked the high beams twice.

"I see you," Marco said. "Get over here already!"

Al didn't need to be told twice. He disconnected the call and sprinted across the puddles in the parking lot to the back door of his dad's car. As he grasped the handle, a dark, tiny hand snaked out from underneath the passenger side and swiped at Al's ankle.

"No!" Al shouted.

A moment later, a tree branch blew out from under the car and across the parking lot.

I'm a mess, Al thought. *Nothing but a frightened, cursed mess!*

Al opened the door and climbed into the back seat of his dad's car, quickly closing the door behind him. As soon as he was safely inside, he locked the back door and lay down on his side. He struggled to catch his breath, but he was happy enough being with his dad and brother.

"Sorry you didn't see us, son," his dad said.

"I didn't even see you in the stands," Al said. "And something was chasing me down the path and—"

"Whoa, whoa," Marco said, cutting him off. "What? What was chasing you?"

Al realized he'd said too much.

"Nothing," he muttered, sitting up. "Never mind."

"Was it an animal or something?" Marco pressed. Al saw his big brother wasn't going to let it go that easily.

"No, no," Al said. "Let's just forget it, all right? I

thought I saw something, but I think it was just a trick of the light or my imagination."

Marco sat back from the steering wheel and turned around in the front seat. His dad spun around in the passenger seat too.

"Well, now I have to know," Marco said. "Don't you, Dad?"

"Well, yes," their dad replied. "What did you see, Alejandro?"

Al groaned. He just wanted to get home, dry off, and sleep for the next month or however long it took for everyone to forget about the past few days. Telling his dad and brother about Robert's curse, or whatever was happening to him, was really the last thing he wanted to do.

"Fine," Al said. "But can I tell you while you're driving home? I'm soaking wet."

"All right," Marco said. "I'm listening."

Al waited a moment as his dad reminded Marco how to put the car back into drive and check his mirrors. His brother was scheduled to take his driver's test in a few months, so he needed all the practice he could get.

"So, remember that doll at the Fort East Martello Museum?" Al began.

As the Padilla family drove off toward home in the dark and stormy night, Al explained what he'd done and what had happened since.

———————

"Why would you do that?" Marco asked as they walked in the back door to their kitchen. "And then tell the doll he's creepy looking? That's like making a bunch of bees angry, then punting their hive through the goal posts."

"Well, that's a little much," Al said, pulling his jersey off over his head.

Number 56, Alejandro "Bad Luck" Padilla, he thought.

"It's all superstition," his dad said, taking off his hat and hanging it on a hook near the door. "If you think you're cursed, you'll act cursed."

Marco tossed the car keys into a basket near the stack of mail.

"I don't know about that," his brother said. "That huge lightning strike hit during the only play Al was in. That's some crazy coincidence."

"Wait," Al said. He sat on a kitchen chair and stripped the sopping-wet socks off his feet. "I thought you didn't believe in that stuff, Marco."

Marco looked at him sideways. "I never said that."

Didn't he? Al thought. He wasn't sure what to believe anymore.

"Then again, I never took the doll's picture or anything. And I definitely didn't call him creepy," Marco boasted.

Al's own voice played his words back in his head: *Smile, you creepy-looking thing.*

"What does this doll look like?" his dad asked. "I've never seen this Bobby doll."

"It's Robert, Dad," Marco said. "You still have the picture, Al?"

I never even looked at it, Al thought. *Even after I took it!*

Al fished his phone from his pocket and navigated to the photo of Robert. There, just as he remembered, was the picture of the antique doll in his sailor hat with the goofy stuffed dog tucked under his arm.

The sight of the doll made Al shudder a bit.

"Here he is," Al said, handing the phone over to his dad.

His dad took a look and was mostly quiet. He made a few grunting noises and then handed the phone back.

"It looks like an old mannequin or something," his dad said.

"A mannequin?" Marco said.

"That's what I said," Dad replied. "Even so, it's not so scary to me."

Yeah, you didn't have one running at you in the rain about twenty minutes ago, Al thought.

"You don't think that doll looks haunted, Dad?" Marco asked.

"Ah," their dad said, putting up both hands as if he didn't want to dirty them even thinking about such things. "It's all in the mind, boys. You make it as scary as you want in your head. Otherwise? It's just an old doll dressed like a sailor man."

"That's what I think," Al said, glad his dad wasn't buying into the curse like everyone else. "Pretty soon things will be back to normal, and everyone will forget about this curse, including me."

"Smart man, my Alejandro," Dad said, wrapping an arm around his shoulder to give him a side hug. "My word, you're soaking wet!"

———

Al stepped out of the shower a half hour later and wrapped a towel around his waist. The hot water made him feel a little better, but more than anything he was glad to be home. He went to the sink and looked into the steam-covered mirror. His distorted reflection looked back at him.

With a hand towel, he wiped the steam clear, fully prepared to see the doll's face appear, probably peering over his shoulder from the tub.

But when he cleared the mirror, Al saw only his own face.

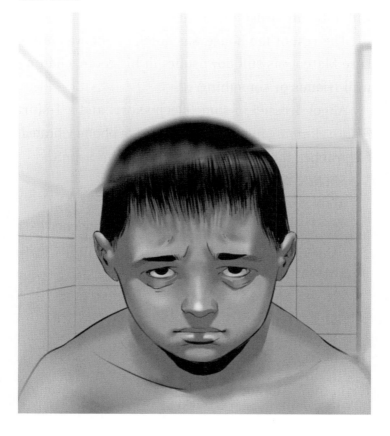

I look exhausted, Al thought, leaning in for a closer look.

There were dark circles around his eyes, and his skin looked paler than usual. His eyes also looked tired, as if it took him a lot of effort just to keep them open.

"All in your head," Al reminded himself.

He found his deodorant and coated both armpits with it before brushing his teeth.

The rest of the house was quiet, but he was pretty sure Marco was still downstairs in his room, chatting with friends or something.

Al got dressed in some sleep shorts and a T-shirt before climbing into bed. As he did, his phone vibrated. He grabbed it and saw he had a text from Selma.

SELMA: **What up?**

AL: **Not much.**

SELMA: **Heard about the game. What happened?!?!?**

AL: **Lightning strike. Lost all the power to the field.**

SELMA: **OMG. U ok?**

AL: **Yep. Blamed once again for being cursed.**

SELMA: **Sorry.**

AL: **Whatever. It's just dumb.**

After sending a few more messages back and forth, they said good night, and Al set his phone on his nightstand. He turned off his lamp and laid his head on his pillow. He stared at the ceiling as the rain continued to fall outside.

Al listened to every creak the house made and the sounds of the storm outside. He didn't hear anything else, no laughing or footsteps. Content that he might actually get a decent amount of rest, he closed his eyes and began to drift off to sleep . . .

His phone vibrated next to him, and the screen lit up, illuminating his otherwise dark room. Al sat up with a start. He reached over to the phone and grabbed it, wondering what Selma wanted.

But there were no text message notifications on the lock screen.

"What the heck," Al said, wiping his eye. He unlocked his phone and saw the photo of Robert the Doll staring back at him.

He closed the photo app, and it immediately opened back up again. He tapped the BACK button in the upper left corner, and it took him to his camera roll. There, in place of every single picture he had taken over the past eight months, were more than four hundred photos of Robert.

Al gasped, his heartbeat picking up pace. "What is going on?"

He scrolled to the bottom of the camera roll and touched the picture. Along the bottom of the screen, he could see the rest of the photos lined up for him to swipe through. Without consciously deciding to, he began scrolling through each shot of the doll. As he did, the doll rocked back and forth in its chair, as if he'd somehow managed to make a mini-movie of the haunted toy.

As Robert rocked in his small, wooden seat, his head tilted up as if to look directly at Al from his plexiglass enclosure. The doll moved back and forth, clutching his toy dog. His beady, black eyes seemed to burn into Al's soul.

Al threw the phone to the end of his bed. It bounced once and clattered to the floor. It went dim as if it had shut itself off.

A quick flash of lightning outside made Al look to the window. As he did, he caught a glimpse of something sitting in the corner of his room, watching him. He felt sweat form on his forehead as his breathing quickened. In a matter of seconds, he felt like he was running laps around the football field yet again.

All in your mind, Al reminded himself. As he said that, the room lit up again momentarily, and he could see Robert's head shaking back and forth.

No it's not, a childlike voice insisted in his head.

Al reached for the lamp, and as he did, his phone lit up and replayed the string of pictures of Robert rocking back and forth. He glanced between the phone and the dark corner where something was watching him.

He clicked the lamp on and cast light back into his room. Almost immediately, the phone went dark. Al turned to the corner and saw a bundle of folded clothes stacked on the chair.

There was no doll at all.

When Al retrieved his phone to look at the pictures, he saw there was only the single shot he'd taken at the museum on Thursday.

The other four hundred or so pictures of Robert the Doll were gone.

CHAPTER 9

BOXED UP

I'm losing my mind, Al thought. *Never mind the curse. The real curse is seeing things that aren't there and believing the dumb things everyone else believes.*

Even so, Al was shaken up enough that he turned on the rest of the lights in his room. He even put on music to keep himself from sitting in complete silence. He would read or watch TV or whatever else he needed to do to keep his mind occupied.

"You're not going to beat me," Al caught himself saying out loud.

Who are you talking to? A voice in his head said.

"Shut up," Al said aloud, then laughed. The noise that came out of his mouth sounded a little maniacal.

Outside, the rain had slowed down a bit. Instead of constantly beating against the windowpane, the rain only occasionally pattered against the glass. It still bothered him that the team blamed him for the lightning strike. He wondered if any of them realized how insane that sounded. Because he didn't ask an antique toy for permission to take his picture, the toy was able to harness the power of Mother Nature and destroy a scoreboard?

From what they seemed to believe, Robert sounded less like a haunted doll and more like a Norse god.

You did call the doll creepy, he told himself.

Al walked around the edge of his bed, trying to keep himself moving and alert. More than anything, he needed to ignore the thoughts in his head. They weren't doing anything but making him feel worse about what was happening to him.

"This will all blow over," Al mumbled to himself.

He stood in front of the clothes on his chair. He studied the pile and recalled his dad asking him earlier to put them away.

How did this pile look like that old doll? He wondered. *It's not even close.*

Considering how terrified he'd been, thinking Robert was watching him from the corner, he began to wish he'd listened to his dad. Absentmindedly, he began hanging his shirts in the closet and tossing handfuls of bundled socks into his dresser. Just to make sure the job was complete, he hung his hat on the knob of his closet door.

There was no opportunity for Robert to magically reappear where his clothes had once been. For good measure, he pulled the closet door closed, remembering what Selma had told him the day of their field trip.

It's weird, Selma said. *It has to be closed.*

Outside his room, there was a creak in the floor that nearly made him dive behind his bed for cover. But then he remembered he shared the house with his brother and dad. A moment later, he heard the toilet flush in the bathroom.

Al smiled and took a deep breath.

What's the plan? he asked himself. *We going to stay up all night?*

"If that's what it takes," Al replied to himself out loud. "I'm done letting that doll and his curse mess with me."

A sudden truth crossed his mind just then.

You do believe it, he thought. *You believe in the curse! Which means you must believe Robert the Doll is haunted!*

"I don't, I don't," Al said. "I swear I don't. It's all just coincidence. This is just my mind messing with me!"

He paced the length of his room some more, thinking about everything that had happened in the past day or so. Most of the "scares" he had were just in his head. He'd never actually seen Robert do anything to him.

As he stepped near the mini-blinds covering his window, he stopped at the cord. It sounded like the storm was over completely. With a quick tug, he tilted the blinds open.

Written in beads of water along the glass were the words *YOU WERE WARNED*.

Al tugged the blinds closed again and felt his hands begin to shake. The small cord in his fingers twitched,

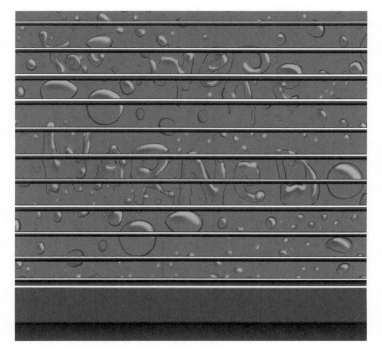

making the beads at the ends of the cords clack together a few times.

I didn't see that, he thought. His heart thrummed quickly as he imagined the old doll tracing its shriveled, worn fingers across the wet window to deliver the message to him. He could just see Robert's unblinking black eyes staring into the window as the doll spelled out the letters one at a time.

"He's not out there," Al reminded himself. "Haunted dolls aren't a real thing, no matter what you think you see."

To prove it to himself, Al prepared himself to open the blinds again. His fingers shook even more, apparently more afraid than the rest of him was.

"Not real," Al whispered to his trembling hand. "Stop it."

As if listening to him, his fingers closed around the drawstring cord and pulled.

The window was clear of any messages. Small droplets from the rain and condensation fell vertically down the face of the glass. It looked exactly like a window still wet from a storm.

Relief washed over Al in a cool wave of air, like stepping into an air-conditioned room after being stuck outside in Florida's humidity. He peered out the window, scanning his wet backyard for any signs of Robert.

Part of him expected the doll to appear from the darkness and scare him half to death.

But nothing happened.

Not wanting to tempt fate, but feeling like his fears were fading, Al closed the blinds. He turned to scan the rest of his brightly lit room. There was nothing out of the ordinary waiting for him. Just his bed, ready for him to climb back in.

Feeling like he was ready, Al walked around to the side of his bed and paused before getting in. There was a movie he'd seen when he was younger that he still thought about from time to time. In it, a stuffed clown had hidden underneath the bed and waited for the boy in the movie to fall asleep. When he did, the clown came out and tried to attack the kid.

Al squatted down and lifted up the blankets to peer under the bed. There was nothing under there but a pair of flip-flops and a tennis racket he almost never used.

There was no clown. There was no doll named Robert, either.

"Good night," Al said to the mostly empty space beneath his bed.

He let the blankets drop back into place and stood up. Turning off all but the lamp on his nightstand, he slid back into bed.

Al lay there for a moment, staring at the ceiling until the pull of sleep got the better of him. Within five minutes, his eyes slid closed and he was asleep.

———————

A short time later, Al opened his eyes. He was sitting up, but all around him was darkness. Something small and soft was pressed against his right side. He couldn't see what it was. His back was sore, as if he was sleeping on a board of wood. Al tried to shift his weight, but he couldn't seem to move.

"Hello?" Al whispered. His voice sounded much louder than he expected, like it was stuck near him.

A moment later, the lights above him illuminated his room. It took his eyes a moment to adjust, but when they did, he could see a crowd of people gathered around, staring at him. The people seemed large, at least twice as big as he was. A pale-faced woman pointed at him, her finger stopping just short of the plastic that enclosed him.

Al looked and realized he was inside a plexiglass cube.

I'm on display, Al thought, panic rising in his throat. It suddenly felt like he didn't have enough air to breathe.

He tried to shift in the wooden chair where he was propped up, but he still couldn't move. The wood pressed into his back, making it throb in pain.

I'm stuck in here, Al realized. No matter what he did, he couldn't move much more than his head. As he did, the people outside continued to point and murmur at him. Nothing they said made sense at all. Everyone sounded like they were mumbling nonsense, making the clear, hard plastic around him vibrate.

"Help!" Al cried. "Please let me out of here!"

An old man with crooked yellow teeth mumbled something to him and pointed to an old camera he had. He waited for a moment before peering through the back of it and squeezing off a shot. A small cube on the camera flashed a bright light, blinding him temporarily.

I can't blink! Al thought, trying desperately to see again. As the panic in him continued to rise, he became increasingly short of breath.

A woman with messy black hair raised a camera at him from another angle. She smiled, revealing a missing front tooth. Just as the old man had, her mouth belched out garbled words before she took a photo of him.

"Please let me out of here!" Al shouted. The noise of his voice bouncing off the inside of his enclosure made his ears ring angrily. "I can't breathe!"

One by one, the faces outside his enclosure changed. He watched as their hair fell out of their heads. Their eyes shrunk to black, shiny beads. Their mouths closed and seemed to seal themselves into a half smirk. Their noses flattened until they resembled nothing more than a bump. Small holes, like passages for worms, erupted across the planes of their faces.

In a matter of seconds, the entire crowd of mumbling, camera-toting humans had been replaced with eighteen animated versions of Robert the Doll.

The doll had Al trapped, sitting in an enclosure just like the one Robert was kept in at the Fort East Martello Museum. The dolls moved closer to the enclosure. They put their strange, flat hands on the plexiglass. Soon, Al was surrounded by Roberts on all sides.

"Get away from me!" Al shouted. "I'm not supposed to be in here! You are!"

The hands began to slap at the plastic cube, making the noise inside almost deafening. The animated

dolls said nothing as they tapped on Al's prison walls, watching him as he struggled to breathe.

I have to get out of here, Al thought. More and more doll faces pressed up against the plastic. They were pushing past one another, trying to get closer. Cameras flashed and hands slapped as if trying to break in and get him.

The soft thing under his arm squirmed. Al glanced down to see the face of Robert's stuffed dog staring back up at him.

"Hey," Al said. "I—"

Before he could finish, the dog snapped at him, baring sharp, jagged teeth. Al cried out in terror.

CHAPTER 10

APOLOGIES

The sound of his own scream woke Al up from his nightmare.

He opened his eyes and sat up, prepared to see an army of Robert dolls lunging at him from the sides of his bed. There was nothing there. Instead, he was stunned to see that it was daytime. Sunlight spilled in through the cracks in his window blinds.

It felt like he'd just fallen asleep. "8:43 a.m.," Al read from his alarm clock. Seeing as how he wasn't sure he could trust it, he double-checked the home screen on his phone and saw that it was accurate.

His thumb left a wet smear on his screen. He was sweating. His T-shirt was soaked, making the fabric stick to his skin. It felt like someone had tossed a bucket of warm water on top of him while he slept.

He wiped his hand on his blankets and then slipped the phone into the front pocket of his shorts.

Al threw back the covers, hopped out of bed, and took two steps to his dresser. He stripped off his T-shirt, tossed it in the hamper, and pulled out a fresh, dry one. As he pulled the new shirt over his head, he heard a childlike giggle coming from the hallway.

What. Was. That? Al wondered, his mind racing for the hundredth time in the past few days. He poked his arms through the holes of his shirt and approached his closed bedroom door. As he did, he heard soft footsteps padding down the hallway.

"Marco?" Al called. "C'mon man. It's not funny."

There was no answer.

Wondering if he might regret it, Al pulled the door open. He gasped at what he saw. There were rolls of toilet paper thrown everywhere. White streams hung from the pictures on the wall. It looked like someone had raided the bulk supply his dad kept in the hallway closet and went crazy.

Robert did it, said the childlike voice in his head.

Al couldn't argue. He was too mesmerized by the scene in front of him. As if on autopilot, he slowly walked down the hallway. His bare feet touched the toilet paper, which stuck to his skin.

The linen closet was open, and towels were strewn about. The place had been ransacked. Inside the bathroom, the shower curtain was in the tub, the medicine cabinet was open, and everything that had been inside it was either in the sink or on the floor. The toilet roll was unspooled onto the bathmat, leaving only the cardboard tube behind.

Everywhere Al looked, there was a mess.

"Dad?" Al called. "Are you home?"

The house was silent, except for a small creaking sound downstairs.

A horrible thought crossed Al's mind just then.

What if Robert did something to them? What if he's hurt my family?

Al ran downstairs and saw their pictures knocked off the wall. The couch cushions were flung everywhere. The television was on, but it was turned to a channel with nothing but static. The black-and-white flecks bounced soundlessly on the flat screen like energized bugs.

"Marco?" Al called again. "Dad?"

He felt woozy, almost sick with the thought that his brother and dad were in trouble. He listened for their voices, hoping to hear a sign that they were okay. As he walked through the dining room, he saw that the chairs were knocked over and the light fixture above the table was swinging back and forth slightly, as if someone or something had been swinging on it.

The kitchen was a mess too. All the cupboards were open, and boxes of cereal, cans of soup, and pasta were strewn carelessly onto the floor.

Al turned and saw the closet near the back door was open a crack.

Is Robert in there? Is he trying to hide from me?

Al took a deep breath and grasped the doorknob.

If he's in there, I'm going to kick him, Al thought.

He pulled the door open. As he did, the phone on the wall next to him rang, nearly making him jump out of his skin.

Al looked and saw the closet was empty. No doll. Just a broom, some cleaning supplies, and a few light jackets.

The phone rang again.

Al grabbed the cordless phone receiver. "Hello?" he said, his voice shaky with fear.

There was a light crackle in the earpiece, followed by the sound of a child laughing.

"Who is this?" Al shouted. "Knock it off!"

The line went dead with a click.

In his pocket, his phone vibrated.

Al set down the landline and fished his phone from his sleep shorts pocket. It was a text message from his dad.

Marco and I went to get breakfast. Didn't want to wake you. Call us when you get up.

"They're okay," Al thought and laughed out loud. Without realizing it, tears began to stream down his eyes. He pressed the button to call his dad. It rang once before the phone went dark.

No, Al's mind screamed. *No way!*

He pressed the power button, but nothing happened. Not even the screen that reminded him to charge his battery. He pulled open a drawer near the refrigerator and fished out a charging cord. Al plugged it into the wall and the other end into the bottom of his phone.

His phone didn't respond.

"I'm sorry, okay?" Al shouted to the empty, ransacked house. "What I did was rude, and I'm sorry!"

That's not good enough, he told himself. *And you know it.*

"Fine," Al mumbled to himself.

He ran past the mess, upstairs through the toilet paper tangles, and toward his room. As he approached his bedroom door, it slammed shut as if a strong wind had just blown through.

Al cried out in surprise. His knew the window wasn't open, especially since it rained last night and they usually had the air conditioning running around the clock. Living in Key West, it was pretty much a requirement.

Almost afraid of what was behind his bedroom door, Al grasped the knob and turned it. He expected resistance but was able to open it easily. Unlike the rest of the house, his bedroom was exactly as he'd left it.

"Let's get this over with," Al gasped.

He went to his computer and woke it up with the mouse. The screen popped to life, displaying his cluttered desktop of files, shortcuts, and photos. Al navigated to the word processing program and opened up a new file.

DEAR ROBERT, Al typed. *I'M WRITING TO TELL YOU*
He paused.

"I can't believe I'm doing this," Al whispered. *Was this really going to help?*

As he sat there, words began to appear behind what he'd written on the screen.

ROBERTDIDITROBERTDIDIT ROBERTDIDITROBERTDIDIT

Over and over, filling up the page, the words appearing faster and faster with every line. In no time at all, the entire page was full of the repeated phrase.

ROBERTDIDITROBERTDIDIT ROBERTDIDITROBERTDIDIT

As Al reached to close the file, the computer winked out as if someone cut the battery power.

Al sat, staring at the black screen.

He's trying to stop me from apologizing! Why?

Al went to his backpack and grabbed a notebook, tearing a piece of paper from it as he hurried back to his desk. He picked up a pen and began to write another letter. As soon as the pen touched the paper, the pen exploded, sending ink all over his hand and covering the paper with blotches of black.

"Stop it!" Al shouted, his hand dripping with ink. He wiped his hand on his shorts, leaving his right hand stained. He pulled open his desk drawer and fished around until he found a red crayon.

Just like my science paper, he thought.

He quickly tore another piece of paper free and began writing a message. As he scribbled out the letters, the crayon broke three times, until he was left with nothing but a nub. Even so, he finished the crudely written letter.

Al held the note up, half expecting it to burst into flames or crumple itself into a ball.

It didn't.

Folding it carefully in half, Al tucked the note into his pocket and dashed back downstairs. He knew what he had to do. He threw on his tennis shoes and ran into the garage to find his bike.

———————

It took Al less than fifteen minutes to get to the Fort East Martello Museum. He raced like his life depended on it—because maybe it did. As he pulled into the empty parking lot, his front tire popped, leaving him to ride on the wheel rim for a few feet.

Al hopped off the bike and laid it on its side near the giant anchor in front of the old brick building. He ran to the front door, grabbed the handle, and pulled.

It didn't open.

"Come on," Al shouted. "Please!"

He tugged again. The door was locked.

Al peered into the building and noticed in the window's reflection that he had some major bed head. He hadn't even changed out of his sleep shorts. His hand was stained with ink, and he looked like a frantic, sweaty mess.

"You can't be closed today," Al said to the building. "It's Saturday!"

The sun-faded poster of Robert the Doll to his left contained a few small cards inside the frame. One of them displayed how much admission was, and another showed the museum hours.

OPEN DAILY 9:30 a.m. – 4:30 p.m.

Al looked around for a clock but realized there wouldn't be one outside. He knew it had been just before 9 a.m. when he'd woken up.

Then I'll wait, he thought and sat down against the wall, just underneath the Robert poster.

After what seemed like an hour, a small pickup truck pulled into the parking lot. A familiar guy hopped out and locked the truck. Al realized it was Corey, the tour guide they'd had on their field trip. He smiled at Al and produced a set of keys.

"Good morning," Corey said as Al stood up.

"Hi," Al said. "I just need to do something real quick."

"You have a letter for Robert, don't you?"

Al pulled the slip of paper from his pocket. "How did you know?"

Corey smiled and unlocked the door. "I've worked here a long time," he explained. "And you're not the first person I've seen waiting to apologize to Robert."

Al sighed and nodded.

"Yeah," Al said, "I didn't ask his permission before taking his picture."

"Happens quite a bit," Corey said.

"I also told him he looked creepy," Al admitted.

"Ooh boy," Corey said and cringed. "He doesn't like that."

"So can I go in and give him the letter?" Al asked.

"Sure," Corey said. "Admission is only nine dollars."

Al felt his heart drop. He didn't have his wallet with him. He patted his pockets as if that would make it magically appear.

"I don't—" Al stammered.

"Hey," Corey said. "I'm kidding. C'mon in."

A wave of relief spread through Al as he walked into the museum.

"If you know the way, go on in and talk to Robert," Corey said.

"Thank you," Al said, reaching to shake Corey's hand.

The tour guide looked at Al's ink-stained hand and shook his head.

"You're welcome," he said, shooing Al away.

———————

Al ran through the museum gift shop and through the empty hallways toward the darkened area where Robert the Doll was on display. He almost wondered if he'd see an empty chair where the doll once sat, considering Robert had completely trashed his house.

Had he? Al wondered.

The usual lights in the display weren't on yet, but there was enough natural light for Al to see anyway. His hands shook as he unfolded the letter he'd written in red crayon. For a moment, he was worried that the note would be blank.

It wasn't.

Al looked at the doll, sitting lifeless and dead-eyed inside the plexiglass cube, holding his small, frightening stuffed dog under his arm.

"Not sure how this works," Al said quietly. He could feel his heart thunder in his chest. "So I guess I'll just read it to you."

The museum was quiet, almost too quiet—as if it, too, were waiting to hear Al's apology.

"Dear Robert," Al began. "I'm sorry for what I did a few days ago. I was supposed to ask for your permission to take your picture and I didn't. I wanted to prove that you were just a doll and couldn't do anything to me. I was wrong."

Al cleared his throat and took a deep breath before continuing.

"I also want to apologize for calling you creepy looking. You're not. I actually think you look kind of cool for a doll that's been around for more than a hundred years. I also like your sailor suit, and your stuffed dog is cute."

Above him, the lights to the display turned on. Al nearly screamed but realized it was probably Corey turning them on for the day.

"I hope you'll accept my apology," Al continued. "I didn't mean to make you mad. I was just trying to show my friends I wasn't scared of you or any curse. I was wrong. Please forgive me, Robert."

Al looked up at Robert the Doll.

"Signed, your friend, Alejandro Padilla."

The museum was silent as a tomb as Al took a step forward. He turned the letter around as if to let Robert read it for himself.

"There you go," Al said. "Are we good now?"

As Al lowered the letter, he could've sworn he saw Robert the Doll nod his head once.

At that moment, it felt like a fifty-pound weight had been lifted from Al's shoulders.

We're good.

AUTHOR'S NOTE

Writing a story about Robert the Doll was kind of a no-brainer. Like Al's friend Selma, I think dolls are scary, so finding a legend about a REAL creepy doll seemed like too good of an opportunity to pass up!

I loved that Robert was donated to the museum by a lady who had kept the doll locked in her attic in Key West, Florida. I'm not sure if she really did hear noises from up there or not, or if Robert even caused them, but it seemed to make sense as to why she had decided to get rid of him.

Based on the research I did about Gene Otto and his infamous doll, I imagined that Robert became infamous around town, even before he became an attraction. Knowing that young Gene blamed anything weird that happened on his well-loved doll, it made me think that word got around about Robert.

I loved that when Gene was older and married, he insisted that Robert have a room with a view. He propped Robert up in front of a window so he could look out at everyone passing by. How creepy is that? Reading that some people claimed to see Robert move or turn his head to watch them fascinated me. To that end, I suspect a lot of locals asked whatever became of the "creepy doll in the window" once Gene passed away and a new owner moved in.

While I've never been to Fort East Martello Museum, I love what they did with Robert. They gave him his own space and even used Gene's famous excuse "Robert Did It" on the poster out front. I knew I had to use ROBERT DID IT at least a few times in this book.

Many people believe the bit about having bad luck if you don't ask Robert's permission to take his photo. Some people claim their lives changed for the worse when they didn't follow Robert's rules. For the sake of the story, I made the things that happened to Al much, much worse!

It's hard to believe an old doll could do so many terrible things from his chair inside a museum, but the legend lives on. If you're in Key West, Florida, stop in and see Robert. Just be sure to use your manners. (And make sure you don't call him creepy, either!)

ABOUT THE AUTHOR

Thomas Kingsley Troupe has been making up stories ever since he was in short pants. As an "adult," he's the author of a whole lot of books for kids. When he's not writing, he enjoys movies, biking, taking naps, and investigating ghosts as a member of the Twin Cities Paranormal Society. Raised in "Nordeast" Minneapolis, he now lives in Woodbury, Minnesota, with his awe-inspiring family.

ABOUT THE ILLUSTRATORS

Maggie Ivy is a freelance illustrator and artist who lives and works in the Ozark area in Arkansas. She found her love for art at an early age and pursued it with passion. She graduated from The Florence Academy of Art in 2010. She loves narrative elements and story-building moments, and seeks to implement them in her own work.

Clonefront Entertainment is a London-based art studio, focusing on illustrations for books and film. Szabolcs Pal, the illustrator for the interior of this series, is one of the fresh talents at Clonefront. He comes from the graphic novel industry, and worked on character developments for movies before moving into book illustration.

DISCOVER MORE

HAUNTED STATES of AMERICA

BY THOMAS KINGSLEY TROUPE

THOMAS KINGSLEY TROUPE

A STARLET'S SHADOW

A CALIFORNIA
GHOST STORY

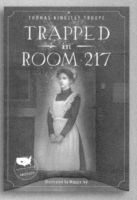

THOMAS KINGSLEY TROUPE

TRAPPED in ROOM 217

Illustrated by Maggie Ivy

A COLORADO
GHOST STORY

CURSE
of the
DEAD-EYED
DOLL

A FLORIDA
GHOST STORY

SWAMP
of
LOST SOULS

A LOUISIANA
GHOST STORY

GHOSTLY
REUNION

A MINNESOTA
GHOST STORY

PHANTOM
of the
TRACKS

A NEW JERSEY
GHOST STORY

BEWARE
the
BELL WITCH

A TENNESSEE
GHOST STORY

SPIRITS
of
THE STORM

A TEXAS
GHOST STORY